See, I'm Still Here

The true story of a very special pet's journey through life

Tom Vuicich

ISBN 978-1-64468-315-6 (Paperback)
ISBN 978-1-64468-316-3 (Digital)

Covenant Books, Inc.
11661 Hwy 707
Murrells Inlet, SC 29576
www.covenantbooks.com

SPECIAL THANKS

I give thanks to God for bringing my wife Margo into my life. Her love and support has been the greatest blessing in my life for over 25 years. Without her, there would have been no Mamma Jean or little Calvin for me to have loved. And of course my dear brothers-in-law, Paul and David, who shared this journey with us.

I also want thank my friend...cousin... brother Jonathan Thielmann. I could not have had this publication produced without his confidential guidance throughout the process.

"Pick me!"
"Pick me!"

The adorable shih tzu puppy was saying when Momma Jean and her son saw him for the first time.

"I want to be yours! I want to be the gift your children give to you."

"Am I the one?"
"Am I the one?"

As Momma Jean looked down at this little guy, she could feel the love. She could feel that he was the one. Although her children were paying for the pup, God was making it happen.

"Yippie!"

"Yippie!"

The little puppy was saying when Momma Jean said, "I want to take you home with me. I want you to live with me forever!"

Hearing those words made this little guy the happiest puppy in the whole wide world!

So off they went, just the three of them.

"What's my name?"
"What's my name?"

The little puppy was thinking as he was being driven to his new home. Then all of a sudden, Momma Jean said, "Calvin, his name will be Calvin. That was my father's name, who is now with God in heaven. But in my heart, he is still here. So now and forevermore, little Calvin, you will be in my heart."

Calvin was smiling from ear to ear and knew he would be loved for the rest of his life.

"I have a family!"
"I have a family!"

It did not take long for Momma Jean and Calvin to become the best of friends. In fact, in no time, they were family. The comfort and joy that they both brought to each other was immeasurable.

"Let's play some more!"
"Let's play some more!"

    Calvin would say each day to Momma Jean. They had so much fun together playing fetch, going for walks, and playing with other dogs. Each and every day they would play.

"I'm growing up!"
"I'm growing up!"

Momma Jean's children saw how the two of them had bonded and could not have been happier for them. They saw how Calvin had grown up with a kindness and gentleness about him that was exactly like Momma's. They could even see it in his eyes.

"Where's Momma?"
"Where's Momma?"

Calvin was saying when Momma's children came to pick him up.

The unthinkable had happened.

Unexpectedly, Momma Jean left earth to go and live with God in heaven.

As sad as they all were, in their hearts, they could hear Momma saying, "I'm still here."

"What happens to me?"
"What happens to me?"

Calvin was wondering, *Where will I live?*

That question was answered when all of Momma Jean's children said, "With me!"

Calvin would now have the best of three worlds. He would live with each sibling for a month at a time.

"Another car ride!"
"Another car ride!"

Each month Calvin would take a wonderful car ride. He always loved his car rides no matter which one of his three new homes he was going to. Each home was different. All were wonderful places filled with fun, friends, and love!

"What fun!"
"What fun!"

Calvin would say each day.
Month after month, year after year after year, he would wake up with one of Momma Jean's children. And although two of the three would be without his company for any given month, they could hear Calvin always saying, "I'm still here."

"I'm slowing down!"
"I'm slowing down!"

Calvin came to realize this when he could not jump on and off the comfy couch anymore. He could not fetch his toy chicken for as long as he used to or run quite as fast. Yet he still had a pep in his step and a twinkle in his eye.

"I'm getting old"
"I'm getting old"

    This is what Calvin was thinking as his hearing began to fail. He was no longer able to hear the door open or his name being called. His vision began to fail as well. He could not chase his toys like he used to. He knew he was not as active as he used to be. But if you looked into his eyes, you could see him saying, "I'm still here."

"It's time to go"
"It's time to go"

Calvin was praying that his family would know when it was time for him to go. Love is the strongest of emotions, and faith in God is love. So because of their love for Calvin, and their faith in God, the family came to see the truth. Even as sad as they would feel, and as much as they would miss him, the whole family came to understand that God was calling to Calvin, and Calvin was ready to go and be with God in heaven.

And so the time did come for Calvin to go and join Momma Jean in heaven. He had given all the love he could possibly give. He had touched more hearts and given comfort to more people than you can count.

So just as Momma Jean's father, Calvin, stayed in her heart and as Momma Jean and her dog Calvin stayed in her children's hearts, remember to be thankful for the good times you had with anyone you have loved who has gone to heaven and know that they will always be in your heart saying, "See, I'm still here."

ABOUT THE AUTHOR

Lying in bed and unable to sleep as Calvin needed eye drops on the hour every hour, Tom came to realize that Calvin's time on earth may be coming to an end sooner than later. This was the catalyst for *See, I'm Still Here*. Calvin's story was written during those sleepless nights. Tom's mother passed away from cancer at the age of fifty-six when he was twenty-four. She left him with two end-of-life thoughts. Number 1, God is love, and number 2 is to never be sad of her early departure but thankful for the twenty-four good years they had together. Tom has kept those two thoughts close at heart, and with Calvin's passing, he was compelled to share his story with all who have lost a loved one.

ABOUT THE ARTIST

Calvin on the Porch the back-cover artwork created by John Danks, a professional artist residing in Bristol, Pa. He specializes in portraiture. He is also known as the artist "buddy" at Children's Hospital where he has and continues to share his art cart to the many kids to lift their spirits. jb.danks@yahoo.com

In Loving Memory of
Mother Jean and Little Calvin

9 781644 683156